This book belongs to

....

For **Beth**, who is *very* good at twirling.

Written by Tim Bugbird
Illustrated by Lara Ede
Designed by Annie Simpson

Copyright © 2012

make believe ideas ltd

The Wilderness, Berkhamsted, Herts, HP4 2AZ, UK.
565 Royal Parkway, Nashville, TN 37214, USA.

www.makebelieveideas.com

Twirly
Pearly

Tim Bugbird • Lara Ede

make believe ideas

Pearly Platt was nearly six

and maybe just like **you**.

She liked to do the kinds of things

most girls like to do.

She liked to *play* and run and sing

and paint and make a *mess*.

But one thing she really **did not** like

was ANY kind of dress!

Then one Monday morning at the beginning of our tale,
a **special card** for Pearly's mom came with the morning mail.

The news was so exciting, she *jumped* up from her chair.

"**Aunt Wendy's getting married!**
You'll need *something nice to wear!*"

Pearly *ran* straight to her room,

not stopping to think twice.

She found her clothes

and **laid them out ...**

nice T-shirt

nice sweater

nice hoodie

nice shorts

EVERYTHING

was **nice!**

nice socks

nice jeans

nice shoes

nice(ish) hat

"I **really** think,"

said Pearly,

"I don't need *anything* more."

But Mom said,

"Put on your boots, Pearl,

we're off to the **party store!**"

Madame Francine's

Madame Francine's *fancy store* was **full** of things to wear,
but not **one** thing with holes for legs – there were only dresses there!

"I absolutely don't like this!"

said Pearly with a frown.
Francine said, "That's nonsense, dear,"
and handed her a gown.

Pearly was **not** happy,
the dress was just **too** *girly*.
But then she turned to take a look
and that's when things got *twirly!*

At first she *spun* a little, and then she *spun* **some more**,
and when she got the feel for it,
she whirled
right through the door!

Belle's Boutique

Beautiful Blooms

Round and round and round she *spun* – she *twirled* along the street.

Mom *ran after* Pearly, but was **knocked** right off her feet!

Fi Fi's Fashions

Nothing got in Pearly's way – *twirling* was such fun!

Just like *flying* (but on the ground) and she'd **only just begun!**

For four full days, Pearly *twirled*

and *spun* just like a top.

She **bumped** and **bashed** and **bounced** about

till Mom cried, "Pearl, **now stop!**

I *thought* the dress was pretty,

but it was a very **bad idea**.

Put it away and no more *twirls* —

do I make myself clear?"

When Wendy's *wedding day* arrived,

Pearly wanted to look her **best**.

"Please, please, pleeease, Mom," she begged,

"let me wear my dress!

I *double* promise not to twirl."

Mom said, "Yes, OK.

But be on your best behavior –

don't **spoil** Wendy's day."

The day was simply *perfect*,
and Pearly was as **good** as gold.
She was Mommy's **little angel**
and did what she was told.

She was as pretty as a picture,
like a **princess** in a book,
but who could guess the
twists and turns
our story **finally took?**

Outside was *bright* and *sunny*,
inside was full of **cheer**.
Pearly said, "Gosh, Mommy,
it's getting **hot** in here!"

The temperature went **up** and **up**
and soon the guests were *dripping*.
The wedding cake drooped to the floor
as its frosting started **slipping!**

Wendy's eyes welled up with **tears**;

she sobbed, "It's all a *mess*!"

Pearly knew the time had come.

She HAD to *twirl* her dress!

Mom just **smiled** and **nodded**;

she was thinking the same thing.

So Pearly started *spinning*

and the band began to **sing**.

Pearly *spun* around the tables – *twirling* as never before – making a breeze that fanned the guests and swept across the floor.

"Faster!" Wendy pleaded, "Do whatever it takes

to keep us cool and most of all . . . **save my precious cake!**"

Pearly whirled with all her might, but the job was just too tough.

Wendy said, "You're doing well, but I don't think it's **enough**!"

So Pearly took the **microphone** –

she knew just what to do –

she called out **loud** to every girl,

"Come join my *twirling* crew!"

They *whirled* and *swirled* together,

each and **every one**.

Pearly's troupe cooled the cake,

and soon the job was **done!**

Wendy *clapped* her hands and asked, "Is there **any** way
I can thank you, Twirly Pearly?

You *saved* my **special day!"**

Pearly didn't think for **long**,
this was the *perfect* chance
to **celebrate** together with a
whirly, twirly dance!